Merry Christmas 2008
Jack and Mike!

Love, Aunt Katie and Uncle Paul

A Flake Like Mike

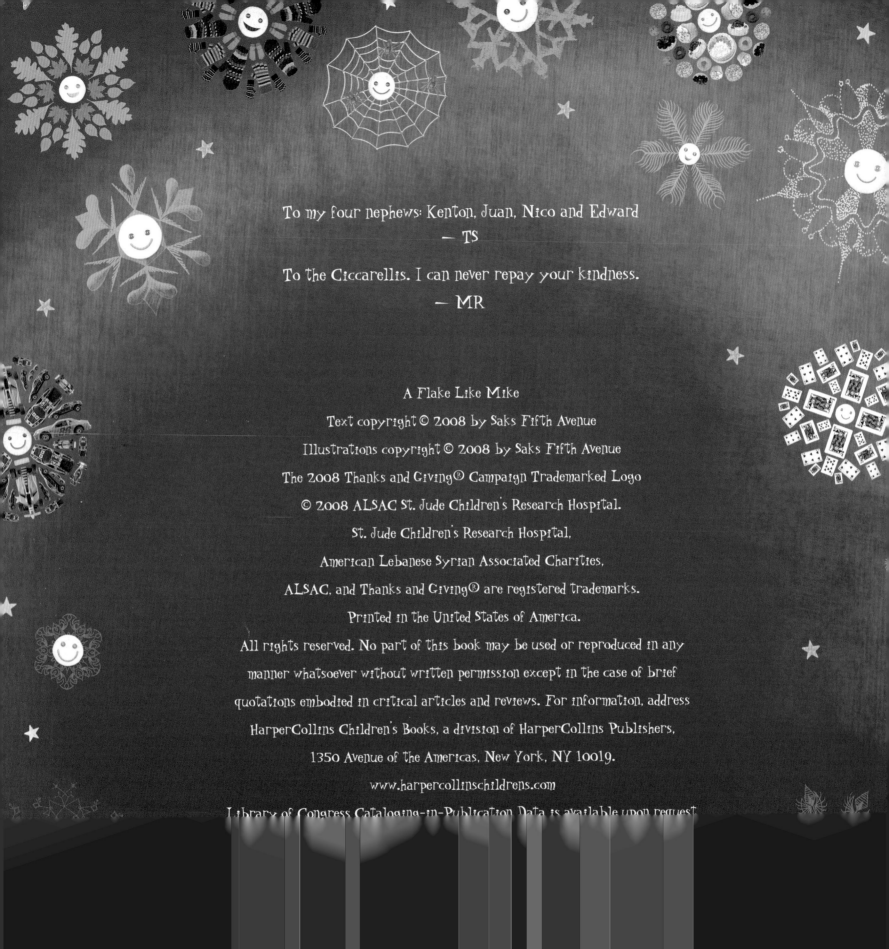

To my four nephews: Kenton, Juan, Nico and Edward
— TS

To the Ciccarellis. I can never repay your kindness.
— MR

A Flake Like Mike

Text copyright © 2008 by Saks Fifth Avenue

Illustrations copyright © 2008 by Saks Fifth Avenue

The 2008 Thanks and Giving® Campaign Trademarked Logo
© 2008 ALSAC St. Jude Children's Research Hospital.

St. Jude Children's Research Hospital,

American Lebanese Syrian Associated Charities,

ALSAC, and Thanks and Giving® are registered trademarks.

Printed in the United States of America.

HarperCollins Children's Books, a division of HarperCollins Publishers,

1350 Avenue of the Americas, New York, NY 10019.

www.harpercollinschildrens.com

Library of Congress Cataloging-in-Publication Data is available upon request.

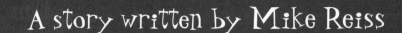

A story written by Mike Reiss

A Flake Like Mike

Saks Fifth Avenue

illustrated by Chris Capuozzo

When your mom and dad were kids
A **BILLION** years ago,
Everything was kind of weird—
Their clothes, their hair... and **SNOW**.

No one much liked snow back then.
It fell in one big **CLUMP**.
It came down fast, it came down hard,
And landed with a
WHUMP!

Neighbor

Sister

Pilot

Father

Mayor

Grandpa

Mailman

Uncle

Waiter

For **SNOWFLAKES** traveled in a bunch and packed together tight. And every one looked just the **SAME.** Six equal sides and white.

Dentist's Brother

Mother

You couldn't tell the boys from girls,
And **FATHER** looked like **MOTHER**.
Sister looked exactly like
Her uncle's dentist's **BROTHER**.

WELCOME TO
Snowflake City
CITY IN THE CLOUDS
ONE SNOWFLAKE IS LIKE ANOTHER SNOWFLAKE
POP. 100 MILLION TRILLION

THEY formed a crowd inside a cloud
And they all looked **ALIKE**,
EXCEPT for one who **DIDN'T** fit—
A little flake named **MIKE**.

The **OTHERS** wouldn't talk to him
Because he looked so **STRANGE.**
Though he'd admit this hurt a bit,
Mike knew he'd never change.
And when they called him **FREAKY-FLAKE**
Mike took it with a smile.
He'd rather **LOOK** the way he did
Than like a bathroom **TILE.**

When winter came, the snowflakes fell
In one **BIG LUMP** together,
Except for lacy little Mike
Who **FLOATED** like a feather.

Mike made **SNOWFLAKE HISTORY.**

(His mother was so proud!)

When it got **WARM**

the snowflakes **THAWED**

And went back to their cloud.

But things had **CHANGED**. The snowflakes asked
How they could be like Mike.
"It's simple," Mike said. "**BE YOURSELF**.
And find a shape you like."

POP!

Snowflake Kate was first to **TRY**
And when she thought it over,
She shut **HER EYES** and she became
A snow-white, six-leaf **CLOVER!**

Then one by one the snowflakes CHANGED—
First TWO, then FIVE, then SEVEN,

A hundred and **TEN**,

SIX thousand, and then

EIGHT TRILLION AND ELEVEN!

One looked like a **SPIDERWEB**

And one looked like a star.

One looked like **SLiMY SNAKES**

(Which seemed a bit bizarre).

Some looked like **TREES**,

Some looked like **BEES**,

Some like flowers and **FLAME.**

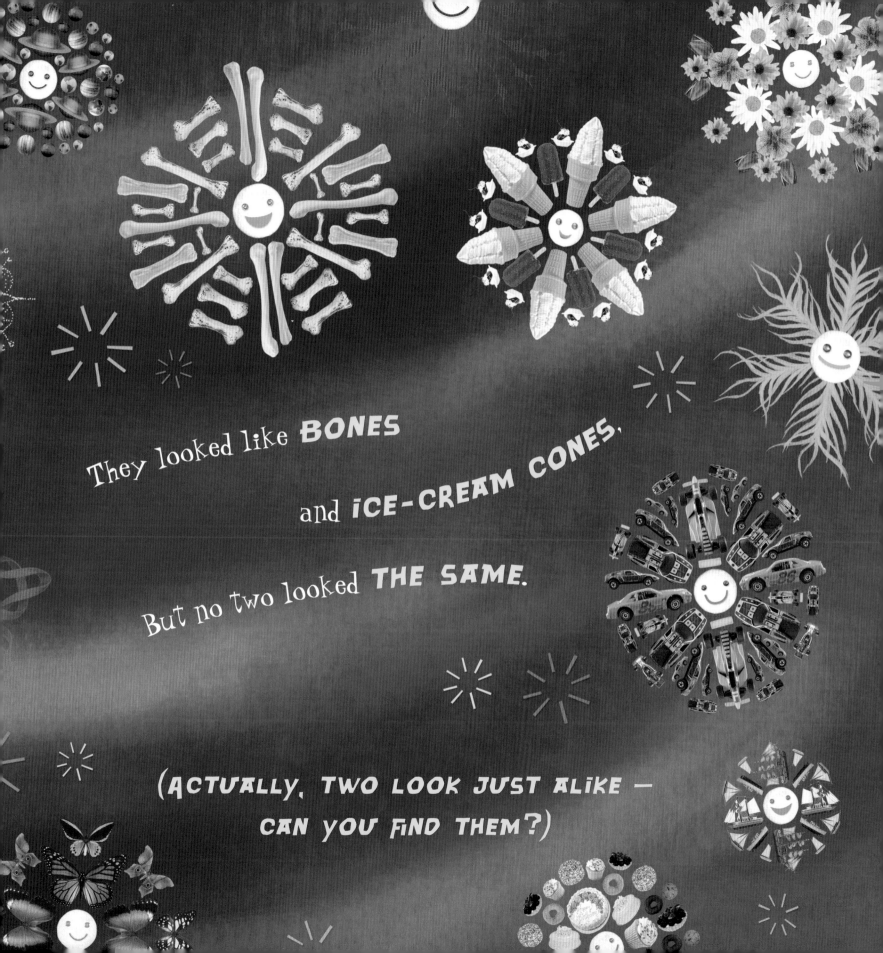

They looked like **BONES**

and **ICE-CREAM CONES,**

But no two looked **THE SAME.**

**(ACTUALLY, TWO LOOK JUST ALIKE —
CAN YOU FIND THEM?)**

When it was time to snow again
Each flake went his own way.

They **FLOATED, FLITTED,
ZIGGED**, and **ZAGGED**

In wintry white ballet.

What a sight! What a **DELiGHT**
To people down below.
They **CAUGHT** snowflakes on their tongues.
They came to love the **SNOW!**

And that's why **SNOW** comes down in flakes

And no two look alike.

And though each snowflake is **UNIQUE**

There's no flake quite like Mike.